I Am the Possibility

Author: Clementina Elba

As I close my eyes, I see the magic inside of me,

I'm not sure how to explain this, exactly.

I see something sparkling way over there,

Oh, it's a crown on my thick, curly, afro hair.

I am a doctor, an astronaut, an engineer,

I see my future ever-so clear.

Actually, maybe a movie star, a journalist

or professional football player.

Doctor
Astronaught
MOVIE
STAR
10
Football
Player

Now, I'm a scientist with the largest magnifying glass,
Ohhhh everything looks humongous and vast.
I smile as I see a trampoline,
Olympic gold is the caption, as I feature
on the front cover of a magazine.

H2O Mg Ca

Magazine
Olympic
Gold

Time to try my hand at a bit of art,
play the flute, steel pans or even the harp.
I can run like Usain at the speed of light,
then welcome the passengers,
onto the night bound flight.

NO1
Athlete
Flight
Attendant

I am excited to imagine all that I can be,
I can dream and be anything, you see.
If my thoughts are in the right place,
I can manifest my dreams, with grace.

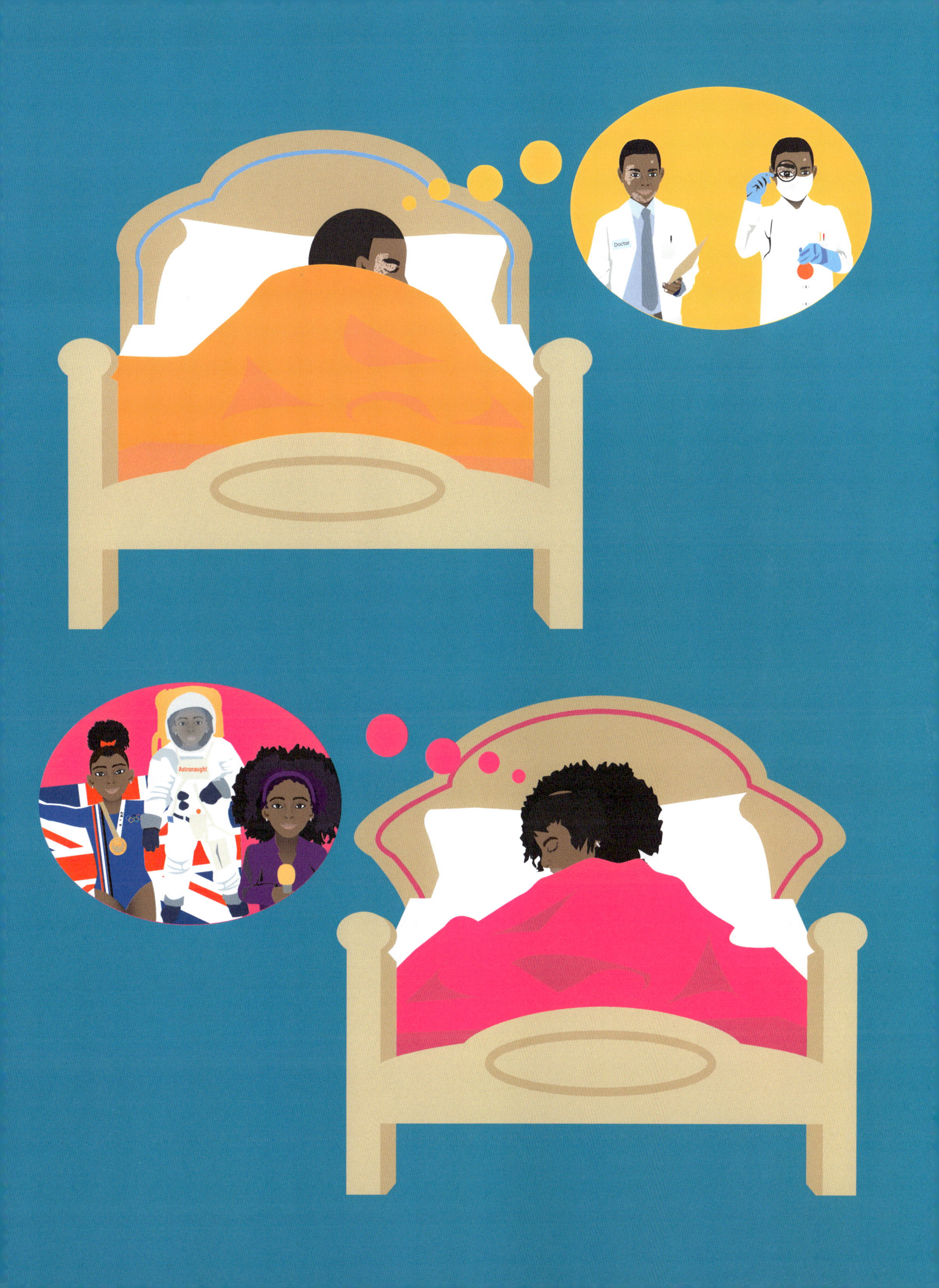

Doctor
Astronaught

As I open my eyes and look in the mirror,

my vision becomes clearer and clearer.

I say; I am smart, I am strong,

I am able and I belong.

I am smart,
I am strong

I am able,
and I
belong

I am loved, I am bright,

I am a truly magnificent sight.

I am the possibility,

the power lives inside of me,

to be just who I want to be.

to be just who
I want to be

I am amazing

I am enough

I am grateful

I am capable

I am helpful

I am determined

I am brave

Printed in Great Britain
by Amazon

19197972R00016